I CAN READ ABOUT

THE SUN AND OTHER STARS

Written by Richard Harris
Illustrated by William Krasnoborski

Troll Associates

Look up . . . one . . . two . . . three stars begin to blink. Then, before you know it, thousands of stars fill the nighttime sky.

But in the daytime, where do they go?
In the daytime, we can see only one star—
the sun. The sun is our special star.

The other stars are still in the sky.
The earth turns. The sun shines brightly and
brings us day. We cannot see the stars, but they
are there.

Yes, the sun is our
special star. It is
a large, round ball
of swirling hot gases.
And it is very important
to us on earth. The
sun gives us the heat
and light we need
in order to live.

The sun is very, very hot. The temperature of the outside of the sun is many thousands of degrees. The inside of the sun is even hotter—much, much hotter.

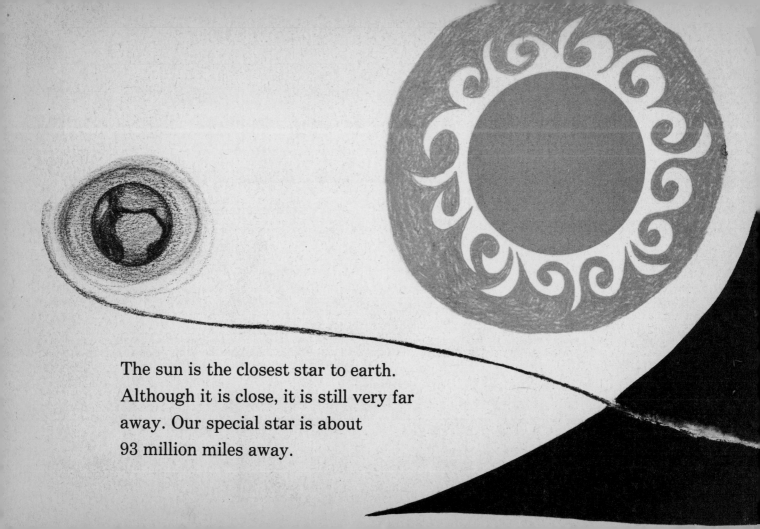

The sun is the closest star to earth.
Although it is close, it is still very far
away. Our special star is about
93 million miles away.

Suppose you could jump into a
rocket ship and visit the next
closest star. It is called
Alpha Centauri (Al-fa sen-TOR-ee).
It is 26 trillion miles away.
Even if you could travel there,
you couldn't get very close.
All stars are hot balls of gas
just like the sun. Nothing can
live on their fiery surfaces.

The sun is the center
of our solar system.
There are nine planets in our
solar system. The earth is the third
planet from the sun. The earth only gets
a small part of the sun's heat and
energy. But it is just enough
to make the earth a very
comfortable place.

MERCURY

VENUS

If we received any more heat, our planet would burn up . . .

Earth

If we received any less, our planet might freeze.

The sun is very important to us.
Long ago the Egyptians and
Babylonians worshipped the sun
as a god.

Even then people knew that the sun is the source of all light, heat, and energy for the earth.

Without the sun, we would have no rain. Plants would not grow.
There would be no food.

Without the sun, our earth would
be a cold, dry planet spinning
through space.

Although the sun is so important to us,
there is still a lot we don't know about it.

Scientists who study
stars are called
astronomers
(as-TRON-uh-mers).
Astronomers use
special telescopes
that let them study
the sun without
hurting their eyes.
These telescopes
take pictures of
the sun.

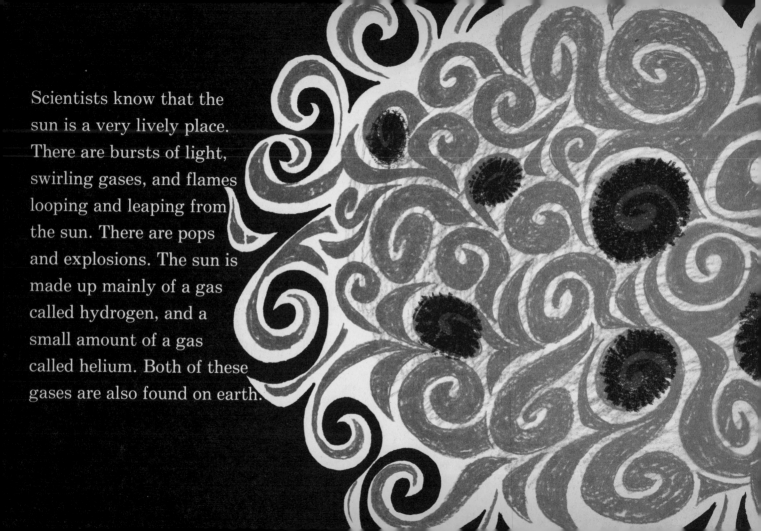

Scientists know that the sun is a very lively place. There are bursts of light, swirling gases, and flames looping and leaping from the sun. There are pops and explosions. The sun is made up mainly of a gas called hydrogen, and a small amount of a gas called helium. Both of these gases are also found on earth.

Gases on the surface of the sun
are always changing . . . rising
and falling all the time. Sunspots
are dark spots on the sun. They
may be caused by gas from the
inside of the sun pushing up
through the surface. Sunspots
are cooler than the rest of
the sun. They are sometimes
100,000 miles wide. Sometimes
they are only a few hundred miles wide.

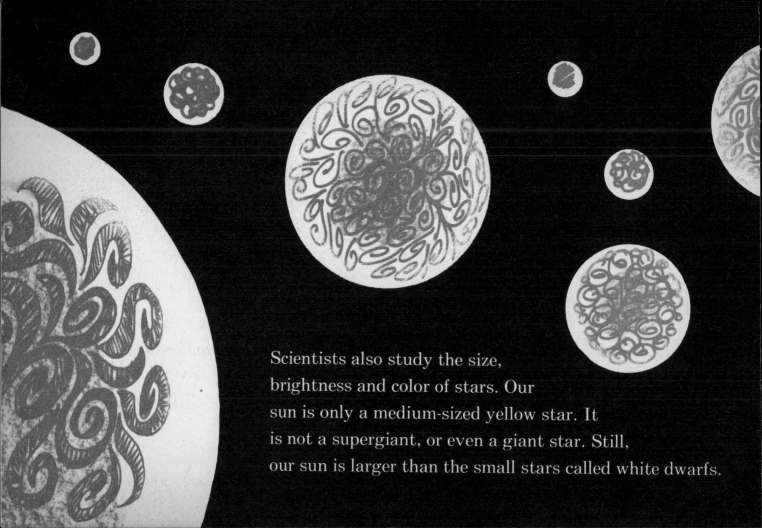

Scientists also study the size,
brightness and color of stars. Our
sun is only a medium-sized yellow star. It
is not a supergiant, or even a giant star. Still,
our sun is larger than the small stars called white dwarfs.

Our sun seems big to us
because our sun is so close to earth.

Our sun is more than a million times larger than the earth. Most white dwarfs are smaller than the earth. They give off a hot, white light.

No one knows how many stars are in the sky.
On a clear night, you can see about two thousand stars.
But there are billions of stars far out in space.
Have you ever looked at the sky and
wondered what is beyond the stars?

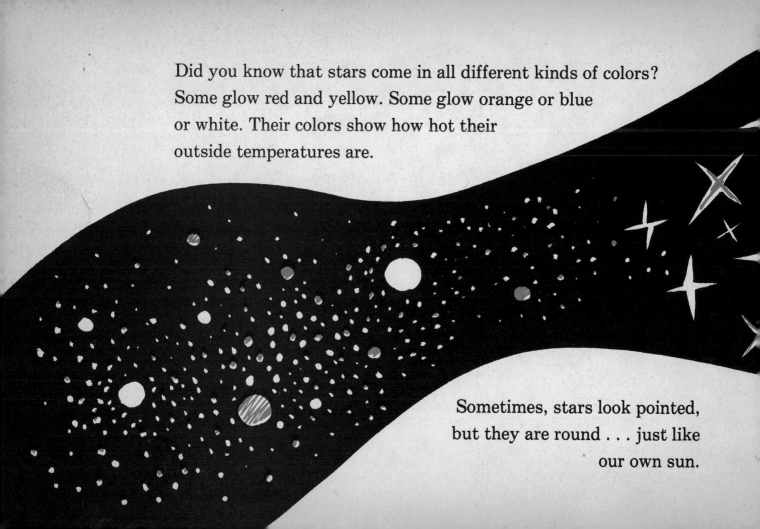

Did you know that stars come in all different kinds of colors?
Some glow red and yellow. Some glow orange or blue
or white. Their colors show how hot their
outside temperatures are.

Sometimes, stars look pointed,
but they are round . . . just like
our own sun.

Sometimes, stars seem to twinkle. But twinkling is caused by air above the earth. As starlight travels toward earth, the moving air bends the starlight, and makes it "twinkle."

People have always wondered about the sky.
Sometimes on a clear night, you can see a
white cloud of dust far away in the distance.

When the ancient Greeks looked at these clouds, they thought these clouds looked like milk. They called them a galaxy. The Greek word for milky is galaxy. Our solar system—with the sun, planets, and stars—is part of the Milky Way Galaxy.

The Milky Way is just one galaxy moving through space. (There are about 100 billion stars in the Milky Way Galaxy.) By looking through a high-powered telescope, you can see another galaxy. It is called the Andromeda (An-DROM-a-da)
Galaxy. It is much larger than the Milky Way Galaxy.
Within the galaxies there are groups of stars that travel together.
These groups are called constellations.

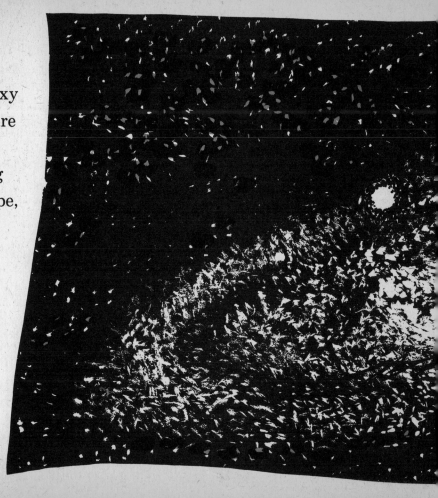

Long ago, some people thought the constellations formed pictures in the sky. What good imaginations they had! They connected the stars with imaginary lines. And they gave the constellations names like Leo the Lion, Orion the Hunter, the Big Dipper. . .

Pegasus the Winged Horse, and the Great Bear.

Look up into the sky one night. Can you find any of these constellations?

We can tell the change of seasons by watching the constellations.

In the winter,
Orion the Hunter is
directly above us.
In the spring,
Leo the Lion is
above us.

Stars are wonderful to steer by.
One star that always seems to be in the same
place is the North Star, or Polaris Star.
It is directly over the North Pole.

Polaris is very bright. It is often the first star you
see in the evening sky. Sailors use the North Star to tell
direction, because they always know exactly where it is.

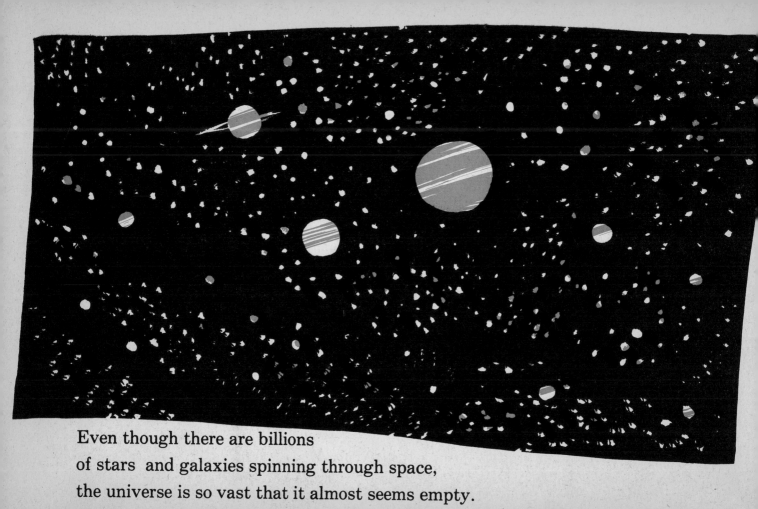

Even though there are billions
of stars and galaxies spinning through space,
the universe is so vast that it almost seems empty.

We know that our sun, our earth and the other planets, and the
billions of stars that make up the Milky Way are only a small speck in space.

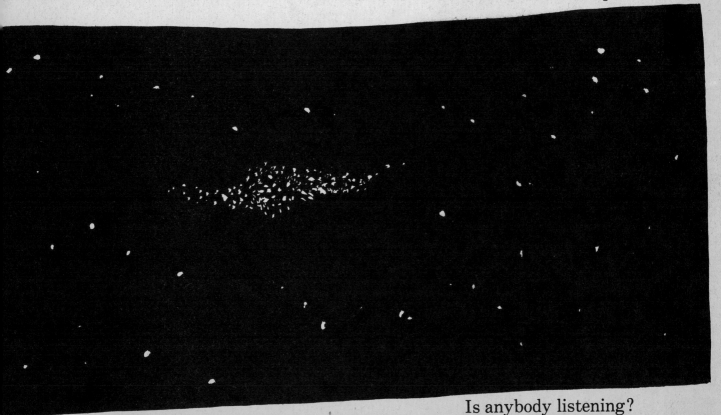

Is anybody listening?

Scientists send out radio signals, hoping
to make some kind of contact in the universe.
They are always looking for new ways
to discover what is beyond the eye
of the most powerful telescopes.

How many stars
are in the sky?

Is there life in
the universe?

How big is space?

Someday we'll find out.
Someday we'll look up at the stars and
learn the answers.
Someday we'll solve the mystery.